ROUGH RIDE

CASS KINCAID

Copyright © Cass Kincaid 2024

All rights reserved.

No part of this book may be reproduced in any form or by any electronic or mechanical means, including information storage and retrieval systems, without written permission from the author and publisher, except for the use of brief quotations embodied in critical articles and book reviews.

This is a work of fiction.

ISBN: 979-8-8693-3722-1

Cover image: Depositphotos

Published in the United States of America by EverLust Books an imprint of Harbor Lane Books, LLC.

www.everlustbooks.com

CHAPTER 1
ISABELLE

"Don't you think for one minute that just because Jace is back with a little money in his pocket and a rodeo title, that it changes a damn thing."

I stare at Emily with sharp, darkened eyes, the usually oceanic blue of them now tainted a cloudy shadowed color due to my obvious frustration at the mere mention of Jace Andrews.

"Call me crazy," Emily says with an amused grin. "But I'd say by your immediate defensive stance that Jace Andrews has you exactly where he's always wanted you...flustered and wrapped around his little finger."

The coffee pot I'm holding begins to shake slightly, betraying the trembling of my fingers. "You take that back right now," I snap at my best friend of over twenty years. "I'm not flustered. I'm just ticked off that everyone I see seems to have only one thing on their minds; Jace and his goddamn PBR win." I set the coffee pot down, which is obviously easier to do than getting my hands to stop shaking. "I'm not saying I don't wish him the best of luck, or that I wouldn't congratulate him on his win if he walked through that door, but I think people around here need to realize that there ain't nothing between Jace and me anymore, so the last thing I need to hear about is him."

"Yeah," Emily says with a roll of her eyes. "You're not flustered at all." She shuffles her way out of the booth she's sitting in—the booth we always sit in when we come to Edna's Diner.

The only difference between our usual evenings spent drinking copious amounts of coffee at Edna's and today is that I'm working, and my shift is due to end in a half hour. "Where are you going?" I ask, unable to see her face now that her hair has fallen like a veil, masking her expression from my view. "I'll be out of here in less than half an hour, if you want to wait."

I take a quick glance around the diner, but it's almost two o'clock, and the lunch rush has subsided, leaving only the regulars and a few latecomers scattered around the room. Nobody seems to be trying to flag me down for a coffee top-up or to complain about god-knows-what, so I turn my attention back to Emily, which is more important seeing as I can't decide whether she's internally laughing at me or starting to get pissed off because I'm snapping at her.

She lifts her head up and rises to her feet, and immediately I know it's the former. "I'm just going to run over to Dan's Auto down the street. I want to see how they're making out with changing that wheel bearing on my car. Having to walk everywhere is total bullshit," she chuckles, pushing her severely straight-ironed chestnut hair back behind her ears. "Besides," she adds, suddenly grinning mischievously as she tilts her head toward the entrance door. "It looks like you're going to have your hands full for that last half an hour, and frankly, I don't want to be around to witness it."

My eyebrows arch up, confused, and I whirl around to follow her gaze. "What the hell are you jabbering on—"

That's when I saw him.

Jace Andrews has just strolled into the diner, accompanied

by Blake and Rodney, his two best friends. They've known each other since childhood, too. Hell, we all have.

And just like Emily and I, they've lived here in Brooksville their entire lives.

But unlike Emily and I, they still believe the sun shines out Jace's ass, and I don't think there's a damn thing Jace could do to ever make them think differently.

Unfortunately, I don't have time to contemplate that or anything else, because Jace has already glanced in my direction and his eyes are locked on me.

I don't want to see him, but I can't seem to look away. And the sight of his chiseled jaw and broad shoulders has me instantly tingling in places I shouldn't be.

He's certainly not trying to hide the crooked grin on his face at the sight of me, either.

"Looks like he's got you in his sights now, Izzy," Emily says under her breath. "Lord help you now, girl."

"Oh, please," I mutter back. I know she's just trying to be funny, but there's a shred of truth to her words. "Even God can't help me now."

I make sure that Jace and his buddies are seated and that Emily has left the diner before I make my way over to the booth they've chosen. "What can I get you?" I ask in the most professional tone I can muster. I hate that he can inflict such pain in me—and such fucking desire—just by being here.

"Well, hey. I thought that was you over there." Jace's eyes are alight with humor. He knows damn well I would avoid approaching this table if I could.

Hell, he knows me better than almost anyone, even Emily. Maybe even better than I know myself.

"It's me," I reply with an edge. "Just like you're still you. Now, what can I get you guys?"

"Feisty," Blake mutters under his breath, and both Jace and Rodney try to stifle their muted laughter.

"I will toss your ass out of this place," I advise him venomously, my eyes burning into him while he tries to compose himself.

"That's enough, Blake," Jace speaks up, but there's still amusement tainting his words, and I hate him for it. "We'll just have coffee for now, Izzy."

His use of my nickname brings me up short. I don't have a good poker face, and I know the fact that it's affecting me is written all over it. I want to curse at him, tell him he has no fucking right to use that name when addressing me, that he's a complete and utter asshole for hurting me the way he did.

But I don't. Not because I shouldn't, but because all I can seem to focus on is how one corner of his mouth is still upturned in a sexy, devilish grin, and how those eyes of his are trained on me, undressing me. In front of everyone. It doesn't make sense, but it's how I feel.

I leave the table without another word, shaking my head to try to rid myself of the erotic thoughts careening through my mind.

I hate what he does to me. What he's *always* done to me.

Jace and I grew up across the street from each other. Inseparable since elementary school, everyone in this godforsaken town expected us to grow up and be...well, Jace and Izzy. Just as we'd always been. He was my first real fight as a kid, and he had the shiner to prove it (that'll teach him for calling me names). He was also my first kiss, my first date, and my first...everything. We'd had it all—the connection, the passion, and the friendship that it was all built upon.

No one ever thought there'd come a day we would go our separate ways.

I didn't, either.

But Jace left me here without him three years ago, chasing his rodeo dream eight seconds at a time.

Guess he didn't think there was room for me in that equation. At least, that's the impression I got when I received the fucking text message he used to break up with me.

You deserve better than the life I can give you, Izzy...

That's it. Dot, dot, fucking, dot. Not even an *I love you* at the end, which is how we'd always ended every conversation, verbal or written. Which showed exactly what was more important to him.

Now, three years later, I've had on-and-off boyfriends, but nothing serious. And Jack over at the Ford dealership that comes here for coffee every morning was nice enough to tell me he'd seen Jace with some bombshell-looking chick on his arm right before the rodeo event he'd attended last summer, wanting to see Jace, the hometown hero, live in action.

Yeah, sounds like he was in action, all right. Getting some action is more like it.

But I don't care. At least, I shouldn't. But fuck if it doesn't eat me up inside just seeing him sitting there in that booth now, giving me fuck-me eyes and licking those lips of his I once loved so much.

Damn it, I think. *This isn't going to end well.*

I place three mugs on a tray and pour coffee into them. I'm behind the counter, an employees-only area, so I don't expect him to be there when I make to turn around. I gasp when his hands press into the counter on either side of me, blocking me in. "What the fuck are—"

"Put the tray down, and don't turn around." Jace's hot breath caresses my ear as he whispers into it, and I feel liquid heat instantly pool within my core at the delicious sensation. I do as he says, something in his voice stopping me from arguing.

"You shouldn't be back here," I advise him weakly. My heart is beating so fucking hard I can barely hear my own voice over it.

"There are a lot of things I shouldn't be," he whispers. I

can feel his mouth against my ear, and my knees are buckling in response to it. "For starters, I shouldn't be over there, feeling like I'm a million miles away from you, Izzy."

"You...I'm not..." I can't get the words out. Jace's fingertips are now tracing painstakingly slow circles on the back of my hand, the one that's pressed against the countertop to steady me. I'm about ready to combust when he drags his teeth against my earlobe, pressing himself into me to hold me upright.

"When do you get off?"

When only a squeak of sound emits from my throat, a suggestive chuckle sounds against my ear. "Work, Izzy. When do you get off work?"

"S-soon," I stammer. "Twenty minutes."

"Meet me in the ladies' bathroom in twenty-one."

CHAPTER 2
JACE

I must admit, watching Izzy fumble her way through the remaining minutes of her shift is comical, even if it shouldn't be. But, it only proves one thing.

Not a damn thing's changed between her and I.

Izzy still loves me, even if I broke her heart by taking so fucking long to come back to her. It didn't do my heart any fucking favors to find out she'd moved on and was dating Chad Easton within a month of me leaving, either, if I'm being honest. But, I get it. I left her here. Served me right to find out she was with someone else.

Part of me really thought she'd wait for me. But seeing as it only took her a goddamn month to sweep me under the rug, she didn't exactly give me a reason to come back before now.

That said, I also saw the way she trembled and heard the way her breath caught in her throat when I pushed myself against her back and nipped at her ear. I'd say she didn't do a very good job of ridding herself of me.

Izzy still wants me, just as fucking bad as I want her.

I won't make the same mistake twice.

I push my empty coffee cup away from me, sending a curt

nod toward Blake and Rodney. "I'll pay for 'em, boys. Now, go on. I'll catch up with you later."

Blake's eyes narrow. "You got something up your sleeve, man?"

"None of your damn business," I reply. It takes every fucking ounce of decency I have not to grin like the fucking Cheshire cat.

"You're going to try to wrangle Isabelle," Rodney chimes in. "Good fucking luck, dude. She hates your guts, it's safe to say."

"I said I'll catch up with you later," I repeat a bit more sternly.

Both Blake and Rodney exchange a quick glance, but they slide out of the booth.

"Like I said," Rodney mutters, holding his hands up in mock surrender. "Good fucking luck."

I watch them leave, knowing how far Rodney's assessment is from the truth. Not only does luck have nothing to do with it, but I also know damn well I don't have to wrangle Izzy into anything. She can pretend to hate me all she wants, but I've already got her, even if she doesn't know it yet.

―――

Ten minutes ago, Isabelle's shift ended. Which means she's nine minutes late.

I'd left a ten-dollar bill on the table, tucked under my coffee cup, and had disappeared into the ladies' room as soon as I was damn sure there wasn't anyone else in there. No one saw me come in, and the fact that there's only a handful of people in the diner and every one of them is male means I can safely assume we'll have a quiet moment to ourselves.

All she has to do is show up.

My courage is deflating more and more with each passing minute, and I'm about to leave when I hear the door open.

Izzy is peeking in through the partially opened door, her eyes wide and wary.

I stand there in the middle of the room, silently willing her to come in of her own accord. *Don't make me fucking beg.*

After a long moment, she steps inside, pushing the door closed gently behind her. The moment the door clicks shut, I close the gap between us and reach past her to flick the lock into place.

"Jace, I don't know—"

"No, you don't."

Then, my mouth is on hers. I don't remember lowering my face toward her, or pushing her up against the wall behind the door, but our tongues are entwined, frantically exploring and searching each other for something neither of us can define. Something neither of us has felt in three years. I'd be narcissistic to believe Isabelle hasn't had her fair share of men and sexual experiences since I've been gone, but judging by the sudden fervor with which she's melding herself to me and grinding her hips against my cock, already straining against the zipper of my jeans, I'd say she's been missing something.

And I *am* narcissistic enough to believe that something is me.

"You left me—"

"Shh, Izzy. Don't think," I instruct her. "Don't fucking talk." I press my rock-hard cock against her, and she whimpers. Such a sexy fucking sound. "We don't have much time, so don't waste it."

To hell with her shirt. I dip my hands under the hem, pulling it up. Just as roughly, I pull her bra down, letting one calloused hand squeeze her breast and pinch her nipple. Another sharp sound emits from her throat.

I kiss and taste a trail along her jaw, whispering in her ear. "Keep quiet, Izzy. You get us caught, there'll be hell to pay."

When I bring my head back to meet her gaze, it's locked on me, and her eyes are wide. For the briefest of moments, there's no sound, no movement, only the pulsing of heartbeats between us. A silent agreement.

Then, Izzy's fingers are fumbling with my belt, unzipping the zipper, and pushing my jeans down over my hips. My cock springs free, and Izzy's unable to keep from staring.

"Oh God." The words tumble from her lips in a sigh, and immediately she reaches between us to touch me.

I clasp her wrist in mine, stopping her just before her fingertips reach their target. "Not a fucking chance," I hiss out hoarsely.

Her eyes are wide, thinking she's done something wrong.

"I've waited too fucking long to have you again, Izzy." My confession pours from me like molten steel. "To hell with the foreplay."

"But—"

I clamp a hand over her mouth, my own eyes blazing into hers. "What did I tell you earlier?" I whisper, my gaze flitting toward the still-closed door and back again. "You're going to get us caught."

I remove my hand only long enough to replace it with my mouth, shutting her up in the most satisfying way I can think of. I kiss her hard, longer than I've ever kissed her or anyone before, desperate to make her breathless and gasping for more of me. When I pull my mouth away this time, I hear the words I've longed to roll off that delicate tongue of hers.

"Oh, Jace...please..."

I'd smile like I just won a fucking prize if I wasn't so painfully hard and aching to bury myself inside her. The sound of her begging me—begging *for* me—breaks something within me. Hell, maybe it puts something inside me back together, I don't know. But I'm lost, consumed by my primal need to have her, to feel the sweet heat of her center enwrapping my cock as I take her relentlessly.

Isabelle helps to undo her jeans and push them down her legs. She steps out of them, and I tackle her back up against the wall just before sliding my hands down her hips and gripping her ass, pulling her up against me. "Hold onto me," I demand through forced breath.

Izzy obeys, hitching one leg up around my hips, then the other.

Such a good girl, I think. *Let's see if I can find the bad girl she used to be with me.*

I drag a finger along her slit, already glistening with her desire for me. Her breath comes out in a ragged breath and her head tilts back against the wall as her eyes flutter, but Izzy doesn't speak.

"Good girl," I whisper out loud. "Now, hold on."

I position myself at her entrance and push, hard, burying myself to the hilt within her. Izzy's mouth opens, and I can feel every inch of her constricting in response. She stays quiet save for the faintest, "Oohh," that falls from her lips.

She feels even better than I remember, if that's possible. I thrust into her, watching in fascination as her eyes squint each time I dive in, and her breath lets go each time I pull back. She's so tight, so wet...so fucking perfect.

"Jesus," I huff, raising one hand against the wall above her head to steady myself, the other still gripping her hip firmly, guiding her to me. Izzy meets each thrust of my hips with a roll of her own, and I quicken my pace.

She's mine. The words tumble around in my head on a continuous loop as I pound into her, one deep thrust after another. *She's fucking mine.* And right now, she is. I own her, every creamy, sweat-glistened inch of her. I fill her completely, unfazed by the rhythmic knocking sound as I slam her back against the wall, or the sinful, muffled whimpers falling from her lips with the pleasure and pain of it all.

I lean forward, using my nose to push her shirt out of the way again, finding her breast with my mouth and sucking hard on her nipple.

"Oh!"

I pull my head back, not once breaking the rhythm as my hips crash against hers.

My eyes are locked on hers. "I told you...not to talk." I can barely speak with the exertion of my movements, but she knows she's made a grave mistake.

I don't hold back, fucking Izzy harder and faster, a relentless, rhythmic bid for release. Hers and my own.

Izzy's bottom lip is secured between her teeth, each sound she makes trapped on her tongue. But her eyes are widening. She can feel my cock twitching within her, my body reaching its breaking point. The tight clenching of her muscles and the biting sting of her fingernails, even through my t-shirt, tells me everything I need to know.

"Izzy." The command in my voice is clear. Her eyes are fluttering and heavy-lidded as she meets my intense gaze again. "Izzy, come with me, baby."

A few more powerful thrusts and both Isabelle and I crash together like a relentless storm, thunder and lightning scorching us from the inside out, our hearts pounding so hard and so fast I can feel hers against my own chest. "Fuck, Izzy, I love you." The words tumble from my lips, against her ear in a fevered sigh as I slow my movements, planting soft kisses against the damp skin just below her ear.

CHAPTER 3
ISABELLE

I'm still breathing hard, trying to calm myself. The color in my cheeks burns, and not just from the inferno Jace has ignited inside me.

He lowers me down onto my feet, refusing to let go until I'm steady enough to stand on my own. I'm shaky and fatigued, but fuck, by the looks of it, that makes two of us.

"Izzy, you—"

"Don't." The word comes out harsh, and it should. Because I mean it. The weight of what I've just done, with Jace, is collapsing the walls around me, and I suddenly feel trapped and claustrophobic.

I hate Jace Andrews. And I've spent three years building up that hate so that I could blast it at him the first opportune moment I got.

Yet, within half an hour of seeing his sultry gaze and muscled physique barely contained under his t-shirt, he's got me half naked, pinned up against my employer's bathroom wall, and he's buried so deep inside me I can't tell where he ends and I begin.

Jesus Christ, what's gotten into me?

"Don't what?" He looks confused as he pulls his jeans back up, buckling his belt. "You've missed me, too, Izzy."

I scramble for my clothes, feeling more exposed and vulnerable than I've ever felt in my life. "Don't," I repeat, doing up my jeans. "Don't call me Izzy." I turn to glare at him, my eyes still burning, but no longer with only desire. Anger smolders there, too. Anger at him, but also at myself.

"C'mon, Izzy—" He reaches out to touch my face as I pull my shirt and bra back in place, but I bat him away.

"I said don't!" I hiss, fighting for the wherewithal to keep my voice down. "Don't call me that! Don't touch me! And don't say...*that*!" I can't even bring myself to repeat what he whispered to me only moments before.

Damn him!

Jace has his hands up in the air now, feigning surrender. "Isabelle," he says evenly, enunciating each syllable. "We need to talk about—"

"We need to do nothing." My tone is clipped. I can barely look him in the eye, smoothing my hair out. "This was a mistake. It never should've happened."

"I beg to differ."

"You would," I grit out, finally bringing my gaze up to meet his. "You shouldn't have come here, Jace. You should've never come back."

He's still standing there as though I've slapped him when I unlock the door and slip silently from the room.

Emily is blowing up my phone. She has been for the past two hours. I haven't been able to bring myself to answer her calls or texts. She's already asked about Jace in three of her five texts, and I know that the moment she hears even the slightest waver in my voice, she'll know damn well something happened between us. I'm just not mentally prepared to admit the truth yet.

Not to her, and not to myself.

I just had sex with my ex-boyfriend in the bathroom of my workplace. Mind-blowing, intense sex. It doesn't seem real.

And it sure as hell isn't right. The biggest problem is that it's not even the amazing sex that's bothering me now.

Fuck, Izzy, I love you. The words had come from his lips with so much conviction, like he had the fucking right to speak them. I can still hear his voice as it caresses my ears, just as I can still feel the ghost of his touch on my skin.

Showering, standing under the hottest water I could handle and scrubbing my body until it stung, hadn't helped.

"Damn you," I mutter to no one. The house I rent from old Addie Phillips is empty except for me and Lucy, my black cat. Lucy glances at me with narrowed eyes from across the room, where she's perched on the back of the couch, basking in the sunlight streaming through the window, glaring at me like I've just interrupted her by speaking out loud.

"Sorry," I say to the cat. I turn back toward the kitchen, intent on brewing a pot of coffee. One quick glance at the clock reminds me that it's almost four o'clock.

To hell with this.

I pull the fridge open and grab a beer instead. "It's fucking five o'clock somewhere," I mumble as I twist the top off, casting a quick glance back toward Lucy. Sure enough, she's glaring at me.

"Oh, stop it. I own you, you don't own me," I remind her. We both know how untrue that statement is.

My phone suddenly lights up on the counter, and I roll my eyes as I take a long pull from the bottle. I know it's Emily again before I even see her name on the display. "You're persistent, if nothing else," I greet her.

"You can't hide from me," she replies. "If it went to voicemail, I was coming over there. I have a key, remember?"

"Remind me to take that away from you."

"Remind me to hide the fucking thing before you get the chance," she chuckles. "Now, why are you avoiding me?"

"I'm not. I'm just tired."

"Bullshit," she replies simply. "What happened? You two get into a scrap? You know if you don't tell me, all I have to do is go into Edna's and someone will tell me what went on. There's always an audience here in Brooksville."

Oh God, I hope not. "Did you get your car back?" I ask.

"Yes, and I'll drive it over there in two seconds if you don't spill whatever it is you're trying to avoid saying. Christ, it's not like you did him on the countertop or something."

Fuck. "Close enough," I admit with a defeated sigh.

"Pardon?" That's got her interest piqued.

"I had sex with him, Em—"

"Jesus! Where?"

"Ladies' bathroom?" I reply weakly, like I'm not sure it really happened. But, it did. It really happened.

There's a pause of silence on the other end. "Holy shit," she says finally. "You and Jace...in the public bathroom at Edna's? Holy fucking shit, Izzy. That's bold, even for you."

I squeeze my eyes shut, willing the alcohol to flood my veins faster. "I really don't want to talk—"

"I thought you hated him?" Emily blurts out.

"I do," I snap, feeling suddenly cornered. "Believe me, I do. But he started saying these things, and then he touched me...I wasn't thinking."

"Damn, girl." I can practically hear her smiling. "That's pretty hot, you know."

"It was pretty something. Not to mention a big freaking mistake."

"Amazing?" she asks. "Tell me it was at least amazing. Got to be worth the inner turmoil I can hear in your voice now."

"It was incredible," I say, far too quickly.

"Damn." Emily sounds like she's living vicariously through me. That's not weird at all.

"Yeah." I clear my throat, downing another mouthful of beer. "So, did you call just for the juicy details, or was there something you actually had to say?"

"Oh, I haven't even begun to ask for details, Izzy." Again, she's grinning; I know it. "But you can tell me in a couple hours."

"What's in a couple hours?"

"I'm picking you up in my car—you know, the one that's no longer howling like a goddamn banshee—and we're going to Tonk's. Live band, cheap beer."

"No way." I shake my head even though she can't see me. "I've got a beer in my hand now, and I just want to stay here where it's quiet. Besides, this house is pure organized chaos." I glance around the room again, sighing. At least, I'm telling myself it's organized. Maybe it's just fucking chaos. "I'm staying home tonight, Em."

"So you can replay sexy time with Jace in your head over and over all night? I'm not letting you torture yourself like that. Get your ass into some tight jeans and wear that low-cut purple halter top you bought last time we went into the city. We're going to dance and drink away the mere thought of Jace fucking Andrews, Izzy."

"Sounds like you're telling me, not asking."

"See, you're such a smart girl. I'll pick you up at eight."

"Em, I don't—"

Too late. She's already ended the call. I stare at the bottle in my hand. Well, it looks like this isn't the only one of these I'll be having tonight.

CHAPTER 4
JACE

In a town as small as Brooksville, there're only two things that are certain. The first is that almost everyone knows everyone else's business. The second thing is that, whatever they don't know, they make up.

Even though Izzy's been unwilling to talk to me for the three years I've been away, I've managed to keep tabs on her, hearing tidbits of information and gossip from my parents and the people from town who'd traveled to different rodeo events to watch me compete. I always asked about her, to make sure she was doing okay, but also in hopes that she'd find out I was still interested. I wanted her to know I still cared about her, even if she didn't care about me.

That also opened me up to hearing the stories and gossip that involved her, true or not. That's how I found out about her relationship with Chad Easton. I had been too cowardly to ask how serious the relationship was, but if the arched eyebrows and inability to meet my eyes were any indication, according to the people I talked to, it must have been pretty serious, especially for everyone to know about it. Not that word wouldn't have gotten around if it was merely a fling, but for it to have been brought up as many times as it was to me, Isabelle and Chad must have been a thing for a while. The last I heard of it was well over a year ago though, and I'd been sure to find out from Blake and Rodney when I got back into town that Izzy wasn't with anyone anymore.

Which meant she was fair game, and that I still had a chance.

And, damn it, I'd taken that chance earlier today. I won't lie, it wasn't my intention when I walked into that diner to send my friends away and get her alone in that bathroom. To say that it was a less-than-ideal spot to have her the way I did is an understatement. But, when I walked in and her eyes locked with mine, I knew I wasn't going to be able to wait. I'd craved Isabelle Thompson for far too long, and seeing her—Christ, she hadn't changed a bit. She was just as gorgeous as I remembered, if not even prettier than my mind had pictured her. She was still beautiful, still fiery, and still passionate as hell in everything she did.

And if the passion and fury between us in that shabby-looking bathroom was any indication, she'd been craving me just as desperately as I'd been craving her.

Or had been, at least.

Now, I'm not sure what to think. Isabelle wanted me in that moment just as badly as I wanted her. And though I don't think she'll even admit it to herself at this point, let alone to me or anyone else, I think that wanting that's been smoldering within her for so long and finally ignited when we came together, that unbridled need that undid her at the slightest sensation of my touch...I think it scared the hell out of her.

She hadn't been expecting it, having chosen to bury it deep within her and ignore it. And for the first time since she'd chosen to ignore it, to ignore how much she needed me, she'd been forced to face that desire, and she succumbed to it, too quickly and too completely.

Now, she needs time. I know that, and I understand that,

but it doesn't make it any easier when the only thing I want to do right now is drive over to that little house that Addie Phillips rented to her last year—Blake told me about it—and remind her once more just how fucking perfect we are together. There's so much we need to talk about, so damn much I need to tell her.

But I can't overwhelm her any more than I already have. Izzy is one of the strongest women I've ever known, and anyone else in this Podunk town will back me up on it. But she's also stubborn as hell, something that I've always loved about her, and she won't be forced into anything. That truth alone gives me hope that the fact that she gave herself to me so willingly earlier today means that there's a fighting chance of me winning her back.

But Isabelle Thompson isn't someone who will be won unless she damn well wants to be.

So, for now, all I can do is do what any self-respecting guy in his twenties does on a Friday night in this sleepy little town.

Tonight, we drink.

I don't plan on getting too rowdy or making a fool of myself like I once might have under the influence of one too many tequila shots, but the thought of chilling out at Tonk's with the guys and listening to the country-rock band that Rodney was going on about today sounds like a pretty decent way to pass the time Izzy needs to come to the same conclusion I've already come to—that we're still meant to be together.

So, I picked up Blake and Rodney and drove to Tonk's bar, telling myself I'd only have one and I'd make sure that the rest of my buddies got home safe. I haven't been around in a long while, so it's the least I can do to let them have a night out and let loose knowing they'd have a ride home when the music ends and last call is unannounced.

The band is good, I'll give them that. Anyone who can

cover a Jason Aldean song that well is okay in my books. I've even managed to nurse the same Budweiser for the last hour without anyone giving me a hard time about needing another one. I've kept my ass plunked in this chair, pulled up to one of the tables in the far corner where I can watch the band play, and amuse myself by watching everybody else get wasted while still being able to shoot the shit with the guys.

And I've been having a pretty good time, too.

Then, two things happen. First, I see Emily saunter through the door, followed closely by a very sexy-looking, very unsteady-on-her-feet Isabelle. The second thing that happens is I see Chad Easton on the other side of the room. I also see his eyebrows shoot up at the sight of Izzy, and a mischievous grin tugs at his mouth.

I could ignore it. Hell, I *should* ignore it. Isabelle isn't mine.

But she damn well isn't his, either.

Which is exactly why I keep my eye on both of them, watching as both girls get themselves a beer at the bar and find their way onto the dance floor. I also watch as Chad pushes and excuses his way through the throngs of people toward her, his eyes set firmly on his target.

I can tell immediately that the conversation between him and Isabelle isn't a welcomed one. At least, not to Izzy. She's drunk, a blind man could see that, but she's still adamantly trying to turn away from him, focusing her attention on Emily and the beer in her hand. Chad, however, seems to be either too buzzed to get the hint, or he's sober and just doesn't give a shit.

Either way, I'm up and out of my chair the moment I see him reach out and grab her by the arm, whirling her around to face him. Izzy's pissed by this point, but her feeble attempt to push him away only results in her intoxicated body swaying dangerously, and Chad uses it to his benefit to pull her closer to him. Isabelle's slurred demand for him to let her go hits my ears just as I push by the last person standing in my way.

"I said get your hands off me, Chad." Izzy's voice is loud, and the people standing close by turn to stare, but I'm disgusted to see that nobody else steps up to help her out.

"I think you'd better listen to the lady," I pipe up. I don't reach out to pull Izzy toward me, but it's a damn strong urge I have coursing through my veins.

Isabelle's eyes grow wide as she takes me in—she obviously hadn't known I was here—but she doesn't say anything. Probably because she doesn't get the chance.

Chad has already turned toward me, a wicked grin on his face as he recognizes me. "Well, well, well, if it isn't the fucking golden boy himself." He might be in the mood to fight me, but at least he's wisely taken his hand off Izzy's arm.

"I don't know about that," I say through clenched teeth. "But I'm pretty sure Isabelle asked you to leave her be. I think you need to respect that."

"You do, do you?" Chad lets out a scornful laugh, looking around as though the other folks around us might find this idea as funny as he seems to be. Thankfully, the crowd that's begun to huddle around us isn't seeing the humor, either. "That's the thing, he adds with a sneer. "I really don't give a shit what you think."

"That's your prerogative, man," I bite out. "But you're still damn well going to care what Izzy thinks."

Chad takes a step forward, and for the first time, I can smell the liquor on his breath. "Or what, Andrews? Are you going to show up and be the one to save the damsel in distress?" He reaches out and shoves me warningly in the shoulder.

I groan inwardly. Not because it hurts, but because this is not going to end well.

"Izzy can look after herself, everyone knows that." There's venom in my voice now. "But there ain't no decent man around here that's going to stand by and watch you manhandle her when she's damn well not interested," I spit out. "Now, do yourself a favor and get the fuck out of here."

"Well, Jesus," Chad laughs hollowly again. "Not only did you ruin things for her when weren't here, but now you've got to show up and prove that you can meddle in things now, too? Shit, you've messed her up so bad she can't even be happy with anyone else." He scoffs angrily again. "Christ, Andrews, you really are an asshole, aren't you?"

My fist hits the son of a bitch's jaw before I consciously make the decision to punch him. A series of gasps and shrieks sound around me, but everyone takes a step back instead of jumping forward to pull me away from him. And that's fine, because it only takes one shot to knock Chad to the floor. And, judging by the way he's cupping his jaw and mumbling out a string of curse words as he lies splayed out, I'd say I don't have to worry about him getting back up anytime soon.

I look up to see Isabelle and Emily both standing there, unmoving, eyes wide as though they can't fully comprehend what just happened. "You okay?" I ask them.

Both women nod their heads, still silent. Which is a bit shocking, seeing as I'm expecting Izzy to rip me a new one over getting involved. But she doesn't. Instead, she says something that shocks me even more.

"I want to go home." The way she's staring at me while she says it tells me exactly what she's thinking, and I just nod.

"I can drive you," I tell her. *I can do whatever you want me to do.*

Emily's eyes narrow, and she looks between us. "Maybe I should—"

I'm not a fool to think that Izzy hasn't told her best friend about what happened this morning between us. They've been inseparable since grade school. Almost as inseparable as Izzy and I had once been.

"Izzy, I'm driving you home." My gaze lands on hers, intense and stern.

She stands there, very still, her eyes burning with defiance. She wants to tell me no. She wants to convince herself that she doesn't want me to take her home.

Finally, with one fleeting gaze over to her friend, she gives an encouraging nod. "It's fine," she assures Emily. "You just got here. I knew I shouldn't have come tonight." She glares down at Chad, who's made it up onto his knees, still cursing a slurred streak of incoherent words, then raises her head to stare at me with glazed eyes. It makes me wonder if I'm not part of the reason she wishes she hadn't shown up. "What about your friends?" she asks me. "I find it hard to believe you came alone."

The corner of my mouth turns up at that. I'm trying to decide whether she's insulting me by assuming I came with another woman after what we'd just done this morning, but, really, it doesn't matter. Because she is even drunker than I thought she was. Maybe even drunker than Chad. She's always been able to hold her liquor well, but her staggering gait and glassy eyes tell me everything I need to know. "Give me two minutes to talk to Blake and Rodney, then I'm taking you home."

CHAPTER 5
ISABELLE

I'd known in the pit of my stomach that it was a bad idea to go to Tonk's tonight. I think my subconscious knew Jace would be there, even if I didn't want to outwardly admit it. Hell, where else would he be on a Friday night? Home, alone? That just wasn't his style.

It was, however, his style to feel he needed to defend me, therefore starting a bar fight without so much as batting an eyelash. If Chad hadn't been so damn—

Christ, how did tonight go so wrong? I was supposed to just go for a couple drinks with Emily, pretend my rendezvous with Jace never happened, and blow off a little steam. Instead, I drank more than a couple drinks before Emily even got to my house, got confronted by Chad for the umpteenth time about rekindling our less-than-stellar romance (just like he does every time he drinks), and ended up standing by while Jace knocked Chad on his ass.

Now, I'm in the passenger seat of Jace's jacked-up Ford pickup, and he's just killed the engine after pulling it into my driveway.

I'm alone with him. Again.

"You're pretty quiet." His voice breaks the utter silence between us.

"My mind is full of a thousand things," I confess. "But I can't seem to think 'em all through."

"I think that's the definition of drunkenness, Izzy."

I whirl around to face him, and everything seems to move with me, making me feel unsteady. "You think you're so funny, don't you?"

Even with the edge in my tone, Jace's smile doesn't waver. "Sometimes. Let's get you into the house."

He pulls open the driver's side door, but I reach across to hold him in his seat. "I don't need your help. But thanks for the ride."

Humor is still glinting in his eyes, even in only the glow of the dashboard lights, but he nods. "Whatever you say, Izzy," he says laughingly. "And, you're welcome."

I have the urge to slap the amused smirk off his face, but I can't seem to get beyond the sexiness of his faintly upturned lips and the heat of his arm radiating through his shirt beneath my fingertips. Even through my muddled brain, one thought manages to make it through loud and clear. *Get out of the fucking truck, Isabelle.*

I do exactly that. No more words, no more glances in his direction. It's safer that way.

At least, I've convinced myself it is until I trip forward while trying to pull my house keys out of my purse at the same time I make my way up the first couple steps of the rickety porch in front of my house.

I careen forward, but I'm immediately caught from behind, two strong arms clasping around my waist to hold me upright.

"Easy now." Jace's voice is soft, encouraging. "I've got you."

My heart is pounding furiously, both from the shock of his presence and the heat now emanating through his chest into my back as he pulls me against him. And, all I can think is, *Yes, Jace. Yes, you do.*

It unnerves the hell out of me.

I fumble to get the door unlocked. The lock sticks sometimes, and I'm too consumed by my plight to avoid eye contact with him to focus clearly on getting the key jiggled the right way to work. Jace's hand covers mine as he takes the key ring from me and opens the door with only a turn of the key and a rough jerk of the doorknob.

I don't reach out to get the keys back, too worried I'll touch him again. Instead, I go inside ahead of him, leaning one hand against the inside wall as I struggle to get my turquoise Ariat boots off. My favorite boots. They're my prized possession, a gift I got from—

"Can't believe you still kept those," Jace says behind me. "I kind of thought they'd have been burned in a barrel somewhere a long time ago."

I get the boots off my feet and turn to face him. Big mistake. Even in the dim light of my tiny kitchen, I can see the smoldering significance within them. The remembrance. "Nah, I love these boots."

"Just like you still love me."

Thank God my hand is still on the wall, because suddenly I'm feeling a lot more unsteady. "You can't love someone when your heart's still broken," I advise him.

"Is that what Easton was going on about?" he asks, taking a step forward, away from the counter he's leaned against.

I can't breathe properly. Damn it, I need another drink. I still feel too much. But, maybe there's not enough beer in the world to make me stop feeling everything the sight of Jace Andrews puts me through. "He said I couldn't get over you. That he was always going to be competing with you, even if it's just your ghost I'm holding on to."

Jace reaches out for me, and I flinch, petrified by the weakness of my body paired with the strength of my desire. "And is he right, Izzy?" he whispers tenderly. "I think he is. You're not over me. Just like I've never been over you."

He has no right to be talking about such things. No right to be standing in my fucking kitchen, taking up the space and air and time I need to distance myself from him again.

But every curse and argument I've got against him disappears in an instant the moment his hand reaches up, his fingers entwining within mine before pulling my hand away from the wall and tugging me toward him.

I don't remember my mouth seeking his out, but his lips are on mine, parted, consuming the last of my control. I melt into him, overcome by the fire in his fingertips as they dive under the hem of my halter top and the hardness he presses up against my belly as he steps backward, pushing me up against the counter.

His tongue steals my breath, no matter whether it's dancing with my own, or licking and sucking a heated trail down my jaw and neck. A sigh escapes my lips, audible proof of how undeniably delicious his mouth feels on my skin.

My hands are under his plaid shirt, grazing my fingernails over the chiseled contours of his lower abdomen, the scalding heat of his flesh making the blood in my veins boil. Jace's breath hitches, and he presses his hips forward, pinning me to the counter. A low, animalistic growl comes from his throat, his own hands tightening their grip on my ass as he grinds against me.

I was right. There isn't enough alcohol in the world to dull my desire for Jace Andrews. He's a compulsion, something my body craves deep within its core, and there's no quenching that craving without having him inside me, losing himself at the same time I'm losing myself.

With no conscious thought, and only my blatant desire to have him guiding my actions, I've got my hands on his belt when his own hands cover mine and squeeze them gently, halting my movements.

"Enough," he whispers. It's gentle, but assertive.

"I want—"

"We both want the same thing, Izzy." He sounds pained. "But be damned if I'll do this while you're drunk. I have higher standards for myself than that, and definitely more respect than that for you."

"But, I'm not—" I whimper.

"Drunk?" He chuckles darkly. "Yeah, and I'm not hard as a fucking rock right now. C'mon, let's get you into bed." He pushes my hands away from his belt, snaking one arm around me to guide me toward the stairs. "We'll talk in the morning, when you're sober."

"I don't want to talk," I mutter, still able to feel the tingling of my skin where his hands had been only moments before.

"Well, that makes two of us," Jace says, still pointing toward the staircase. "But, there's a ton of things that need to be said. Now, let's get you to bed, before I change my mind."

"So, there *is* a chance you'll change—"

"There's no chance," he snaps, but there's a hint of laughter in the way he says it.

"Then why say there is?" I whine dramatically, taking one stair at a time and concentrating on not falling flat on my face.

"Because it gives you something to think about." He grins, stepping up onto the stairs behind me, his hands placed suggestively on my hips. He leans forward and nips playfully at my shoulder, making a strangled combination of a gasp and groan erupt from my throat. "Sweet dreams, Izzy."

The sun is bright. Way too damn bright. My first thought is that I'd forgotten to close the curtains on my bedroom window before I went to sleep last night. But my next thought quickly erases that one from my mind, and my eyes snap open as I steal a glance around the room.

I'm in my bedroom, and thankfully I'm alone. I take a deep breath, relieved. I remember very clearly that Jace brought me home last night. I also remember how much I drank, and the way my tongue had meshed so enticingly with his as we stood in the kitchen downstairs, albeit briefly. While I don't remember him winding up in my bed last night, I know all too well that doesn't reflect how badly I'd wanted him to. Sober or not, Jace Andrews still had the ability to strip me of my control with the slightest fleeting glance.

And I don't like it.

I groan as I slide out of my bed very ungracefully. Somehow, the coffee pot seems a million miles away right now, despite only being a short distance away in the kitchen downstairs. It's on the tip of my tongue to mumble out a few choice words about my decision to drink the way I did now that I'm dealing with a dull ache in my head and a serious feeling of dehydration. Christ, it's not like I didn't know any better. About the alcohol, and about Jace.

But that urge is quickly killed as I make my way with heavy steps down the stairs and around the corner into the kitchen. From there, I can see the sleeping form stretched out on my couch. I'd recognize those broad shoulders and Wrangler jeans anywhere, and it stops me in my tracks.

Jace.

I have half a mind to shake him and wake him up. The memory of him punching Chad has just drifted to the surface of my mind, and I feel justified in cursing him out for thinking he needed to create such a scene like that.

But only for a moment. Because the bigger part of me is relieved. Relieved that there's someone else out there who wanted to defend me, even when I didn't need to be defended. And relieved that the Jace Andrews I fell in love with so many years ago still exists, the one who wants to protect me and put himself smack dab in the middle of conflict for me for no other reason than so that I don't have to contend with it. It's soothing to know that he still feels strongly enough for me to have gone up against Chad like that, no matter how misguided his actions might have been.

Again, it occurs to me that my actions were just as misguided, and still are, and that I need to remember the pain and heartache Jace put me through. But my train of thought is quickly derailed.

"Anyone would be able to hear you coming down those stairs, Izzy. Were you purposely stomping your feet to wake me up, or still buzzed enough to not realize you're doing it?" Jace rolls over on the couch, his smug smirk already plastered across his face, despite his sleepy, half-lidded gaze.

"I didn't realize you were here," I say defiantly, though my heart's pounding at being caught staring at him. "I thought you'd have gone back to wherever you came from."

It's a harsh thing to say, but, damn it, he's being cocky already and I haven't even had my first sip of coffee yet. "Why didn't you go home?" I ask, trying to soften my tone a bit.

Jace sits up, running his hands through his hair and then down over his face. "I don't know," he admits with a shrug. "I just didn't want you to be alone in this house. I haven't been around in a while, but I still know you enough to know that you've always handled your alcohol pretty well and might've been drunker than I maybe thought you were."

"So, you're telling me you stayed in case I was shit-faced?" I contort my face disbelievingly. "Just wanted to watch the show, in case I ended up with my head in the toilet bowl?"

"Jesus, Izzy, it's not like that." Jace stands and smooths out his wrinkled t-shirt. "I just told you, I didn't want you here alone. And if you had ended up getting sick, at least I'd have been here to help you through it."

"How noble of you," I bite out.

Jace steps toward me, and at first I think he's going to try to envelope me in his arms. I flinch despite the fact that he's a few steps away, and if he notices, he doesn't say anything.

He passes by me and heads into the kitchen. "Another thing I know about you," he says over his shoulder, "Is that you're not a morning person. Never have been. And obviously, not a damn thing has changed."

I let the veiled insult slide, turning to watch him curiously. "What are you doing?"

"Making coffee," he says simply. "By the sounds of your surliness, you need it."

"I can make my own coffee," I state. "I don't need you to do it for me. I'm fine. I'm not feeling sick, and I've only got a headache to remind me of how stupid I was last night. So, you can go. You don't have to be here babysitting me."

Jace is just filling the coffee pot with water. At the sound of my declaration, he turns the tap off and whirls around to face me, one eyebrow arched high. "Wow," he scoffs. "I'm not sure whether to be more offended that you deem some of the things said and done last night as you just being stupid, or that you're dismissing me like being here is some dirty little secret."

"You know as well as I do that half the town will have seen your truck in my driveway by now, Jace," I inform him, crossing my arms in front of me. "I can just hear the fucking rumors now." I hope I seem more confident than I am.

"So, you don't want me to leave, per se. You just don't want anybody else to know I'm here."

"Don't read more into this than there is," I snap. "Everybody probably already knows by now that you punched Chad and made that big scene at Tonk's last night, so your truck still being parked in my driveway this morning is not going to help the rumor mill."

"To hell with what people say," Jace replies, now sporting

an edge in his voice as well. "They'll always find something to talk about, you know that."

I run my hands through my hair, frustrated as hell. Not only by Jace's blatant argumentativeness toward me, but also by the fact that he's right—I don't want him to leave. And that is *exactly* why he has to. "You're not listening," I stammer. "I really do think you should go."

"Speaking of going, where exactly are *you* going?" Jace's gaze flits around the room, and for the first time, I take in the fact that he's staring at the disarray of my living room and kitchen, cluttered with cardboard boxes and totes in various stages of being packed up.

Damn it. "I'm moving."

Suddenly, Jace is eerily still in front of me, and only the sputtering of the coffee pot is heard in the room. "You're moving," he repeats, as though testing the words on his tongue. "Where?"

His tone makes it sound like I'm doing something wrong by even suggesting such a thing. It makes me *feel* like I am, too. "Frankly, it's none of your—"

"Where, Izzy?"

I huff a loud sigh. Everyone in town is eventually going to find out anyway. "Los Angeles."

Jace doesn't even bother to try to hide his surprise. "Los Angeles? Izzy, that's halfway across the damn country."

"Thanks for the geography lesson."

"But that's not even just a city. That's a massive city. Christ, they'll eat a small-town girl like you alive out there!"

"Gee, thanks for the vote of fucking confidence." He's got my hackles raised now.

"Izzy, you can't—"

"I'm pretty sure you don't have a say in the matter," I interject angrily. "You forfeited that three goddamn years ago."

There it is. The hurt and fury I'd pent up over the years, finally directed at the man who caused it.

"I didn't—" Jace seems tongue-tied, unsure what to say, or do. "Christ, Izzy, how have I not heard about this before now?"

"No one knows. Just Emily. And judging by your reaction, I should've kept it that way."

His hands are raking through his hair like the movement is keeping him somehow grounded. There's a sense of inner turmoil rolling off him in waves, which seems hardly justified to me considering he's the one who left me here, not the other way around. "When?" he asks finally.

"When what?"

"When do you leave?" His eyes sweep around the room again, as though the answer lies amidst the chaotic mess.

"Next week," I reply, pushing by him to get a coffee mug from the cupboard behind me. "And, frankly, the sooner, the fucking better."

CHAPTER 6
JACE

She may as well have socked me in the gut with the weight those two little words held.

I'm moving.

"Isabelle, you can't move next week." It's blunt and to the point, but it's the fucking truth.

"The hell I can't," she snaps back, glaring at me before purposely turning her back on me to pour herself a cup of coffee. "I don't know who you think you are—"

"You know exactly who I am," I remind her.

She shoves the coffee pot back onto its base, then carefully sets the mug down. Her hands are trembling slightly, although from anger or another emotion, I can't tell. "Wrong," she advises me. "I knew who you were. Once upon a time. But you destroyed that silly fairy tale, didn't you?"

Her eyes are blazing. In all the years I've known her, I'm not sure I've ever seen such blatant ferocity coming from those depths.

"You don't get a say, Jace," she continues. "I've been in this godforsaken town my entire life. It's time to get out of it. Away from the bullshit, away from all the memories…" She blinks, then locks her gaze on mine. "Away from you, and every memory of you."

I swallow down the bile rising in my throat. It sickens me to think she hates me enough to leave her hometown. Our hometown. "Izzy, you obviously didn't believe me back then, but I told you...I told you I would come back for you—"

"No." She barks the word at me, pointing a finger in my face. "Don't you dare, Jace Andrews. You didn't say that. What you said was, '*You deserve better than the life I can give you, Izzy.*' I should know, believe me. Those fucking words have haunted me for three goddamn years."

Another punch to the gut without even touching me. "Wait. I did say that—"

"You're damn right you did!" She shook her head. "And over a fucking text, no less."

"Wait, no. Izzy, shit." My thoughts are jumbled, and I can't seem to make sense of them. "You *did* deserve better than what I could give you back then—"

"And I deserve more than you now, Jace." Her fiery gaze is back on me, and I'm convinced I can see the pulse beating wildly in her throat. "You came back too late," she adds. "Way too late."

Something's not adding up. But, unfortunately, I can't think straight. I'm losing her all over again, and the realization is slicing through me with the red-hot pain of a knife. I can't lose her again. I won't.

Isabelle must think I've chosen not to respond, and she averts her gaze, reaching for her coffee cup on the counter. I take my chances, reaching out in one fell swoop to pull her to me, crashing my mouth down onto hers. The desperate need to remind her of what we are and what we've always been together is all-consuming. I kiss her like my life depends on it, and in a way it does. The life I want—the life I came back for—is slipping through my hands.

For the briefest second, I feel Izzy succumb to my kiss, her knees buckling as she leans into me despite her surprise. But it's over just as quickly as it began, and she pushes me away, hard.

"Jesus, Jace, what the hell's gotten into you?" Her fingertips come up to touch her bottom lip gently, as though she can still feel my kiss. "You can't just use the fact that I can't seem to control myself around you to your advantage."

A sharp twinge of satisfaction buzzes within me at her confession. Her obvious breathlessness and the uncertainty in her voice boosts my ego, too. She's not even sure of what she's saying, so I don't feel compelled to be, either. "You admit it, then."

"It doesn't change things."

"Izzy, it changes everything!" I bellow, once more exasperated that she can't seem to understand that we're still the same Jace and Izzy we've always been. Or, maybe she just doesn't want to. "Because it means that not a damn thing has changed. Not where you and I are concerned."

She's staring hard at me, unsure what to do or say next. I'll admit, I've got a few damn good ideas, but I give her time. That's the thing with Izzy, I'll give her everything she wants, if she'll just let me.

She is quiet long enough that I start to feel like I've actually made progress, like she's actually weighing the things I've said in her mind. Then, finally, "It's too late, Jace."

"It's not." There's not a beat of hesitation in my reply.

"It's too late," she says again, nodding as though attempting to convince herself. "You need to go."

"Izzy, I'm telling you—"

A loud knock makes the walls of the old house shake, and we both snap our heads toward the door. The sight of her is marred by the gauzy translucent curtains on the door's window, but I recognize Emily there, nonetheless.

"Shit," I mutter under my breath. I turn back to Izzy, standing at the counter. She looks shell-shocked, like she's been caught doing something she shouldn't have been. Or someone. I guess that'd be me. "Izzy, I swear to God, I never meant to hurt you the way I did. There's been a misunderstanding—"

Her hollow, angry laughter stops the desperate string of words coming from my mouth. "A...misunderstanding?" She laughs again, but there's nothing humorous about it. "You shattered my heart, Jace. There's nothing to misunderstand in that." She points to the door. "Now, as fun as this little trip down memory lane has been, you need to leave. I'm asking you, Jace. Please, just go."

I take a step toward her, but Izzy immediately puts her hands up between us, blocking me. "Izzy, it's not what you think. If you just—"

She blinks rapidly; the tears are burning her eyelids, threatening to fall. "It's exactly what I think," she replies in a thick voice. "It's over."

This woman has the power to hurt me in ways I never imagined. Hell, I'd thought I'd been gutted by her three years ago when she chose to change her phone number and start dating Chad. That feeling of desolation doesn't even begin to stack up against what she's putting me through right now.

I don't say another word, instead choosing to take a giant step away from Izzy. I'll give her space between us. I'll even give her a moment's reprieve. But time, that's what I'm running out of. So, I give her a sad smile and a nod before I leave, knowing my chances are limited to make her realize the truth—that this, *us*, Izzy and Jace—we're the furthest thing from over.

All this time. Three goddamn years.

Izzy spent that entire time hating me for the fact that I broke her heart. And, by the sound of it, that's exactly what I did.

This thing is, I've spent the last three years wondering why she broke *my* heart and cut off all contact with me. I mean, I thought I knew, and that's exactly why I didn't storm back into Brooksville and fight for her the way I should've. Because I was a coward, and because I was hurting pretty damn bad. Thinking that the woman I loved had chosen to move on without me when the only thing I'd tried to do was build a better life to offer her…

Yeah, I was pretty torn up. She'd broken my heart, and bruised my ego pretty fucking bad, too. So, I'd made the ridiculous choice to back down, back away, and let her have what she wanted. Freedom. From me, and from the dreams we'd once had together.

Except, my dreams finally came true—I rode one bull after another, all the way to the top, and I won the Professional Bull Riders World Finals.

I became a world champion, and I didn't have Izzy by my side to share in the celebration with me. Now that I know it's because of something so fucking stupid, the pain of that fact rocks me to my core even more. So much time wasted, when we could have been together.

That's why I'm here, outside Davidson's Hardware. Emily's father has owned it as long as I've been alive, and his father owned it before him. Everyone here knows that. Another thing that's a well-known fact is that Emily's father, Hendrick, doesn't drive. Not since the collision that happened ten years ago that almost cost the man his life. Since then, he's never been behind the wheel of a car. And since then, Emily has dropped him off at the store in the mornings on her way to work at the post office, and she's picked him up every evening.

She doesn't deviate from that schedule today. I'd said

absolutely nothing to her this morning as I passed her on the way out of Isabelle's house, but the heavy, curious look she gave me spoke volumes. She didn't hate me, even if her friendship with Izzy dictated that she, in fact, should. Which is why I'm taking a chance, hoping she'll hear me out, even if Izzy won't.

Judging by her narrowed eyes as she climbs out of her Corolla, however, I wonder if I've made an error in my calculations. I climb out of my truck and slam the door. "I need to talk to you, Emily."

"Well, hey, Jace. Good to see you, too."

"Sorry." I hold up my hands in surrender. "My manners aren't nearly as important to me right now as this situation with Izzy."

"Situation." She scoffs, laughing darkly. Damn it, I wish she and Izzy would stop doing that. "You can't just show up here after almost three years with a big fat paycheck in your hand and think Izzy's going to run back into your arms after what you did to her."

I want to argue that that's exactly what she did, but now isn't the time. "I've made my fair share of mistakes, I won't deny that. But, Emily, there's something she doesn't know. Hell, it's something I didn't know until this morning. But, my biggest mistake will be letting her run off to Los Angeles without at least explaining it to her."

Emily's forehead crinkles in confusion. "You broke her into pieces," she says after a long pause. "Are you saying there's more to it than that?"

We're standing on the curb in front of the store, and I don't care who hears me. "I'm saying I never intentionally broke up with, or hurt, Izzy. Just like she didn't hurt me the way I thought she did." My chest is pounding furiously against my ribcage, and all I can do is pray that she'll listen to me. "And I can prove it."

Emily stares into my eyes, obviously trying to determine

how much of my story is utter bullshit. Whatever she sees, it makes her sigh. "Shit," she breathes out. "Fine, give me a couple minutes to get Dad, then you can follow me to their place. I'd say we could go to Edna's, but Izzy's working, and if I walk in there with you, she'll kill us both."

CHAPTER 7
ISABELLE

Waking up to find Jace in my living room had been a rough start to the day. And it sure as hell didn't get any better after that. I couldn't focus. In the span of my eight-hour shift at Edna's, I'd managed to spill a cup of coffee, get three orders wrong, and forget to bring condiments and utensils to a couple of tables. I wasn't on my A-game, and my mind wasn't on the tasks I needed to accomplish.

My mind was on Jace. Not just on the way his eyes spoke to me, enticing me and burning into my skin. Or the way his tongue ran across his bottom lip as he drank me in with his gaze. It wasn't even the way each muscle and contour of his hard chest and shoulders stretched the fabric of his t-shirt.

No, it's his words that have me faltering.

Not a damn thing has changed. Not where you and I are concerned. You're not over me. Just like I've never been over you.

Damn it, one more week and I'd have been gone. I would've never had to face the likes of Jace Andrews again. Instead, he rides back into town and consumes me just by being close enough to breathe the same air. He doesn't just create chaos for me, he *is* chaos. I want to hate him for it, the way I've told myself I did for the past three years.

But wanting to hate someone, and actually hating them are two different things. And seeing and feeling and thinking about Jace makes me feel a lot of things, but hate isn't one of them.

Yeah, I hate *that*, too.

I can't wait to get home and hide within the deepest depths of my house. I'll lock the door, draw the curtains, and medicate my overwhelmed brain by tossing a frozen pizza in the oven and watching Netflix while I drink a beer. I should be packing, but to hell with it. The mental warfare going on inside me is winning, and just for tonight, I'm going to allow myself to drown it out with mindless entertainment and carbohydrates.

But when the clock strikes ten o'clock and I turn around to find Emily smirking devilishly at me from the other side of the counter, I groan out loud. "No," I tell her immediately. "Whatever you have planned, I'm not going to be a part of it, Em. No, no way."

She laughs, rolling her eyes. "Oh, please. You don't have to be so dramatic. It's not like we get into trouble every time I have an idea to liven this town up a bit for us."

I shove a handful of napkins into the dispenser on the countertop, glaring at her. "People have been stealing glances and whispering in here all godforsaken evening about Tonk's last night. And those that didn't whisper, flat out fucking asked," I admonish, even though it's not her fault.

"Asked what?" Emily's eyebrow arches.

"About Jace and I."

"And what'd you tell 'em?" She leans forward, grinning from ear to ear, whispering, "Did you tell them how you two desecrated the bathroom?"

"Shut up," I hiss, looking around to make sure no one's paying attention to us. "Jesus, what's gotten into you? I mean it, I'm not going out with you tonight. I need a quiet night at home."

"Alone?"

"Yes, alone!" I slam the dispenser in my hand down onto the counter with a bang, huffing a sigh. "I'm on the verge of a mental freaking breakdown, and you think this is funny."

"I don't, I swear." Emily holds up her hands in mock surrender. "I don't think the fact that you're about to have a breakdown is funny at all. What I do find funny is that Jace has you all hot and bothered, and yet you won't admit it to yourself, let alone me. You need to think about why he's affecting you like that, Isabelle."

Her use of my full first name brings me up short. "I'm not getting into this here," I say, my voice clipped.

"You haven't gotten into it for three years," she shoots back. "Trust me, you should have."

I push the napkin dispenser out of the way, crossing my arms. "What the hell does that mean? And why do you sound so damn cryptic?" I'm agitated, and anyone other than Emily would've told me to cool my bitchiness by now. "If you have something to say, Em, just say it."

Emily's crooked little grin is back in place as she slides off the stool and swipes her keys off the counter. "The only thing I've got to say is that I know something you don't, Izzy. And, as your best friend, I'm telling you that I'll be in the parking lot, waiting. Get your ass out into the passenger side of my car as soon as you're done cleaning up. You're going to want to hear this."

She turns away from me and slips out the door of the diner before I can say anything more, tugging on the chain to turn the Open sign off as she goes.

"This better be good," I snap, fumbling to buckle the seatbelt. Emily's already squealing the tires on the way out of the parking lot. Wherever she's taking us, she's in a big fucking hurry to get there. "Christ, slow down, Em. You drive like a lunatic on a good day, but this is erratic, even for you."

"Desperate times call for desperate measures, my friend."

"Okay, enough with the theatrics." I rake my hands through my hair. "Tell me what it is you think I've got to know."

"I can't." Emily's eyes never leave the road in front of her, but that purse-lipped smile of hers is back in place. "I have to show you."

"Oh, Jesus Christ," I mumble, rolling my eyes. "This is ridiculous."

"Maybe, but you'll thank me."

"I doubt that." I don't even turn to look at her, instead focusing my gaze on the darkness out the passenger window, longing for my night of Netflix and beer. "Can you at least tell me where the hell we're going?"

"The Point."

That catches my attention, and I whirl around to face her. "What? Why the hell are we going there?" I hadn't been to The Point in years. Its actual name is Barlow's Lookout, but teenagers have always used it as a place to go to make out, smoke up, and do all the things that parents warned them against. It happens to hold a little more significance for me than just a make-out spot, however.

"You'll see."

I'm silent as Emily drives beyond the town limit and turns onto Barlow Road, a winding, gravel road with a steep uphill slope. It may have been years since I was out here, but the path that leads to that spot hasn't changed a bit, and it's conjuring up ghosts of memories that are better left buried.

She turns the car into the clearing at the top of the hill. It's wide open, just as it's always been, and the lights on the water tower on the other side of town seem to cascade out over the town's expanse. Only two other cars are parked there, and one's not actually a car at all. It's a truck.

A familiar truck.

"Emily, turn the car around."

"Not a fucking chance, Izzy." She parks her car away from the other two vehicles—it's customary to try to give other attendees of The Point as much privacy as possible. "Sorry, but this is for your own good."

My mind is spinning, a confusing mix of anger and shock that she'd do such a thing. "Tell me you didn't just bring me here because he asked you to." I'm glaring at her with every ounce of fury I can muster, but it doesn't begin to express the turmoil rolling inside me.

She kills the ignition, and the resulting silence is deafening. "I told you, there's something you need to know."

"Then fucking tell me, Em."

She shakes her head. "I didn't say you were going to hear it from me," she says apologetically. "Now, put your big girl panties on and get out of the car."

"Emily—"

"I know, I know. You should hate me, blah blah blah. But you won't." She reaches across in front of me, first unbuckling my seatbelt, then pushing the car door open. "You'll thank me. Go."

I feel like I should argue with her, tell her this was underhanded and uncalled for. But I make the mistake of glancing out the window, and I can see Jace standing there, hands in his pockets, about fifteen feet from the car. He's waiting for me, and he looks nervous.

Good, I'm glad I'm not the only one. Because I know that Emily would've never agreed to deceive me like this if that *something* I'm about to find out isn't big. "Son of a bitch," I breathe out as I clamber out of the vehicle.

"Love you, too," Emily calls out right before I slam the door.

She's started the car and is peeling out of that clearing before I even have time to register the way Jace's eyes are set firmly on me.

"Remind me to rip her a new one for this later," I say. I'm trying for a dash of humor, but the shakiness of my voice betrays me. I clear my throat and shove my hands into my denim jacket pockets, matching Jace's stance. "Tell me why I'm here."

"I can do better than that, Izzy," he says gently. "I can show you."

"I'm getting really tired of hearing that."

A glint of confusion shadows his features, but Jace doesn't say anything more. Instead, he chooses to pull his phone from his pocket.

My first inclination is to notice how banged up the damn thing is, with its screen cracked and the case held together by a strip of duct tape, but the fact that he holds it out to me prevents me from commenting on its state of disrepair. "I don't want your phone, Jace."

"Yes, you do." His arm stays extended, the phone held out toward me. "Take it. I need you to see something."

I pause, hesitant, but I reach out and take it from him, careful not to let our fingers touch.

"The passcode to unlock it is 0107."

Immediately, I know those are the numbers of my birthday, the seventh of January, but I don't say it out loud. I'm too engrossed in whatever's about to happen. I can feel the weight of it, thick between us. I punch in the digits and the screen lights up.

"Go into my text messages," Jace instructs. "Scroll all the way to the bottom. You'll see your name there."

Why the hell would my name be there? That's my first thought. The second is that he was obviously sick and twisted enough to keep the damn message he sent me. A new wave of molten fury floods my insides, but I do as he says, scrolling to the bottom of the text messaging screen. Sure enough, my name is at the very bottom—the oldest messaging conversation in the list. I click it, and it's on the tip of my tongue to snap at him, asking him why the hell he's doing this, bringing all this hurt and pain back to the surface.

Then, I realize something. The last message in the conversation isn't the one I think it is. I know I never responded to Jace's last text message to me, the cruel one that ended everything between us.

Except, that's not the last message he sent me.

The message that's haunted me for three goddamn years is there, and it hurts just as much as the first time I read those words on my own phone screen. *You deserve better than the life I can give you, Izzy...*

But another message shows up after it. *And I plan on building you the one you deserve. Please wait for me. I love you.*

According to the time stamp on it, it was sent the same day as the previous one. I can't breathe as I press my thumb against the screen and hold it there in order to view the message details. All the air is gone from my lungs, and my throat has constricted so tightly I'm afraid I might suffocate from my own sense of disbelief.

Both messages were sent within a minute of each other.

But I never received the second one.

My head snaps up, and I gaze at Jace with widened eyes as the realization begins to sink in. "You...didn't break up with me."

"And you didn't wait for me." There's no malice in his tone, only resignation as he offers me a sad smile.

The pain behind it breaks my heart, when I thought it couldn't be shattered anymore. "I didn't get this message," I explain feebly, holding the phone out as though it's proof.

"I realized that this morning," Jace states. "Far too late,

obviously. All this time, I thought *you* broke up with me. Decided waiting for me wasn't what you wanted. Yet, the entire time, you—"

"Thought you broke up with me," I finish for him. "Over a fucking text message." I sound defeated, and that's exactly how I feel.

"I never would have done that to you, Izzy." Jace takes a step forward, his eyes firmly set on me. "And if I had ever been stupid enough to break up with you, I'd never have done it over a text message."

My mind is whirling with so many thoughts, so many questions, I'm not sure which to ask first. "All this time," I breathe out. "Lost. Purely because I—"

"Turned your phone off and changed the number the next day." Jace smiles again. "Emily told me she was with you when you got the first text. I know how much it hurt you to think I…did that."

There's pain in his voice, and I feel guilt slice through me, knowing my actions are the cause of it. "Emily told you everything, then." It's not a question. I can see the truth on his face. His jaw is tight, and his eyes are shadowed. He knows.

Jace just nods. "She told me you…retaliated. With Chad."

The blood drains from my face. Seeing him look so pained, and sound so lost—it's killing me. "It was a stupid, drunken night about a week after I got your message," I explain. "One drunken night that somehow led to eight months of pretending to be more than we were."

"You ended up dating him." Jace shrugs, his hands still in his pockets. "There's no shame or blame in that, Izzy. You thought we were over. Hell, I dated the PBR's public relations advisor for a while, too, but…"

Jace trails off, and it's my turn to chuckle sadly. "But it's like wine after whisky."

A crooked grin forms on his mouth. "*Exactly* like wine after whisky."

I swallow down the lump in my throat, holding his phone out to him. "Jace, I swear—"

He reaches out for the phone, bypassing it completely and grabbing onto my wrist, tugging me against him. His mouth finds mine without consciously having to seek it out. The connection between us, the tangible pull; we'd be able to find each other in absolute darkness. The warmth of his tongue against mine sends a shiver of hunger straight to my core, and I kiss him back with just as much intensity and promise as he offers me.

"I thought the distance and the time away from here had become too much for you to handle," he whispers when he pulls away, his forehead pressed against mine as his fingers cup the side of my face. "I've always ended every conversation with the truest words I know, Izzy—I love you. Remember?"

I nod against him, feeling the heat of tears welling up in my eyes. So much emotion was pouring out of me, and the closeness of him after so long of being away from the familiarity of his tender kind of touch was only exacerbating the tsunami erupting within me. "I know." My voice is hoarse, and it cracks under the weight of the tears that spill onto my cheeks. "I should've never—"

"Shh." Jace's fingertip comes up to rest against my lips. "No more apologies, and no more regrets, Izzy. There's just one thing, okay?"

I sniff as he wipes a stray tear from my cheek. "And what's that?"

The corner of his mouth quirks upward, and he leans forward, kissing me softly. "The most important thing," he says, as though reminding me. "I love you, Izzy."

Three years I've waited for the sound of those words on this man's lips. Over one thousand days. Except, I didn't know I'd been waiting. Too much hurt and pride and anguish shrouded my heart to realize it. Now, the words mean more than they ever have before. Because the path he took to get here, to be with me, to say those words, is winding and confusing.

But it has led Jace here, despite everything. Back to me.

I smile against his mouth as I kiss him again, tucking myself into him as close as I can. "I love you, too," I whisper. "And I'll never let you forget it."

"Oh, I won't forget," he promises. "Just like I won't ever forget our nights out here." He doesn't pull away, but turns to look out over the bluff. The town lights twinkled and blinked, as though answering back. As though they remember just as much as he does. "Remember, Izzy?"

Mischief comes alight in my eyes, and I smirk knowingly. "If this old clearing could talk…"

"Let's be thankful it can't."

"How come?" I tease. "Don't want it to tell everyone about the mix of silky promises and dirty words you spewed?"

"I don't give a damn what they heard, Izzy," he whispers. "It's what they saw. Back seat of my truck, front seat of my truck…Christ, the bed of my truck…"

I stifle a soft laugh, then kiss him softly, nipping at his bottom lip suggestively. "I'm not sure I remember what you're referring to," I whisper softly. "Maybe you should remind me."

"I can't do better than that," he assures me, tugging me toward his truck by both hands. "I can show you."

CHAPTER 8
JACE

Four months later...

"Izzy." My voice was soft and soothing. "Izzy, wake up." I pulled the sheets down just enough to slip my hand beneath them, letting my fingertips caress over the soft swell of her hip, across her lower abdomen.

"Izzy…" I say again, this time in a more taunting tone. She's lying on her side, away from me. My fingers find their mark, moving through the soft hair at the apex of her thighs. The heat I can feel emanating from her is enough to make my cock twitch suggestively against her back.

Being naked with Izzy in her bed is something I never thought I'd experience again. Needless to say, every chance I get—hell, every chance we both get—we're hidden away inside this decrepit old house Izzy rents, sharing more private, sensual touches and whispers than I have any right to deserve.

Pride, on both our parts, almost destroyed us indefinitely. We have a lot of time to make up for.

I roll my hips forward, pressing my erection into her back as I dip one finger between her soft folds. A soft gasp comes from Izzy's lips, and I watch as her eyes flutter.

"Jace…" It's the faintest sound, but it's coupled with her legs opening slightly, giving me more access.

I stifle a guttural groan of my own as the sight of her sleepy form and the sensation of her damp warmth on my fingers consumes me. I slide my finger over her clit, finding my way inside. Jesus, she's so wet, yet barely awake.

"Oh, Izzy…" I breathe against her skin. It's so fucking hard to control myself around her. My mouth is on her shoulder without conscious thought, kissing and sucking and licking a trail up to her throat, where I can feel her pulse speeding up.

She moans again, eyes still closed. Her hips rock slightly against my hand, easing my finger further inside her. I begin to move within her, in and out, slowly at first. I can see Izzy's hand slide under the cover to the edge of the bed. The realization that she's gripping it only encourages me.

I withdraw my finger, painstakingly slow, relishing in the soft whimpers Izzy emits. Her clit has my attention now, and she arches her back against my cock. Another groan falls from my lips, sounding more like a growl, a sign of weakness.

"You're so wet," I whisper against her ear. "I want you to come for me." I tease her relentlessly, flicking and rubbing with the pad of my finger until I see Izzy's eyes clamp shut.

"Not…yet," she pleads.

I know what she wants, and my mouth quirks up at the sound of her begging me for it. She wants my cock buried deep within her, pounding her until she screams my name in desperation as her body shatters beneath me.

Hell, I want that, too. She's insatiable. And fucking gorgeous. But I like having a little control over her, giving her what she needs on my own terms. And, right now, all I want is to make her come hard from my touch.

I swing one leg over hers to hold her in place. "I said I want you to come for me." My breath is hot and damp against the side of her face, and the sheets are bunched up where her hand is clutching the side of the mattress. "Come, Izzy," I command her. "Come hard."

My finger is rubbing wildly against her now, and only labored, desperate panting is coming from Izzy's mouth. That's fine, because I don't need her words. Her body is telling me everything I need to know. I can feel the muscles in her legs and back tightening as she tries desperately to ward off her impending climax.

"I want you…" she pleads on a sigh.

"Not…until…you come." I suddenly stop my sensual assault on her clit, making Izzy's eyes snap open and a gasp passes her lips. Her slick wetness makes it easy to plunge two fingers inside her, and Izzy cries out at the intense sensation.

"This is what you want?" I growl against the side of her face, thrusting my fingers in and out furiously. "You want me to fill you, baby? Push you over the edge?"

"Yes," she gasps desperately. "Oh, god, yes."

I can feel how tightly she's clenched around my fingers. Izzy is close. I hold her in place, and I'm relentless as I stroke her, in and out, hard, fast. Every fiber of her being is taut and on the verge of losing control.

"You feel amazing, Izzy," I encourage. "Give in, baby."

"Oh, god, Jace—"

Every muscle of her body, inside and out, constricts violently, her walls tightening around my fingers as she explodes beneath my touch. I don't halt my movements until I've milked every last shudder and convulsion from her body.

She's breathing heavily, her body now limp and exhausted as I slide my fingers out slowly and gently, tugging her close to me. My arms envelop her, and I nuzzle my nose into her neck, grinning as she squeaks in response. I know her too well; every nerve ending in her sexy little body is still on high alert, and the slightest caress or tender touch still feels intense and erotic to her.

"Good morning," I whisper against her skin.

"Good morning, yourself." She lets out a dramatic sigh, sinking against my chest. "That's quite the way to wake me up, you know."

"That doesn't sound like a complaint," I chuckle, planting soft kisses just below her ear.

"Believe me, it's not." She wriggles slightly, purposely pressing her back against my evident hardness. "What about you? I've got a few ideas—"

She's already rolling over with mischievous intent in her eyes, but I grope for her wrists, holding her in place. "Not so fast," I chuckle. "There's time for that later."

"You always say that," she whines. But she's grinning like the Cheshire cat.

"Izzy, there is rarely a time I've ever stopped you from putting your hands on me," I remind her.

"That's not what I mean." She rolls her eyes dramatically, like I'm the one misunderstanding this predicament. "I just mean that you always say that. That we have more time. Like you know for certain."

"That's because I do." I lean over, tackling her to playfully pin her underneath me. "I won't ever lose you again. Time is on our side now." I kiss her, hard, then mentally chastise myself for getting sucked into another potential sexual escapade with her. "Damn it, Izzy, I can't keep my hands off you." I roll off her like the heat of her skin is scalding me, theatrically holding my hands up in the air as I stand. I'm naked before her, and very, very hard.

Izzy's got a lopsided grin on her face as she sits up, holding the sheets up to cover her chest. "You say it like it's a bad thing."

"It is. Right now, anyway." I turn my attention to the floor, looking for my jeans. "Especially since I have a surprise for you."

"I'll give you a surprise, if you'll come back to bed."

That's enough to make my head snap up, and Izzy's staring at me like I'm something she wants to devour. Shit, she's incredible. I point a finger at her. "Stop it," I smirk. "You're killing me over here. Now, get out of bed. I've got something I want to show you. You can put your hands anywhere you want after that."

"Promise?"

She looks so innocent when she asks, but I know better. "I wouldn't say it if I didn't mean it, Izzy. Now, get up. I'll meet you in the truck in fifteen minutes."

Normally, Izzy resembles a zombie in the mornings, using only a series of grunts and head movements to convey what she needs until the coffee kicks in. But whether it's the excitement of not knowing where I'm taking her, or the sexy, impromptu way I woke her up this morning, she seems wide awake and alert. I'll have to keep that in mind for future reference.

A travel mug of coffee is cupped in her hands, her hair still damp from the quick shower she took before getting dressed and climbing into the truck like I'd instructed her to. No makeup, no fussy hairstyle.

She looks breathtaking, and I keep stealing glances at her from the driver's seat. She might be excited, but I'm a nervous wreck on the inside. My nerves are shot, and they have been for days. Either I've done a bang-up job of hiding it, or Izzy just hasn't noticed. Maybe she just has and hasn't said anything.

"You're really not going to tell me where we're going?"

"Not a chance." I reach across the console, pulling one of

her hands away from the travel mug to entwine it with mine. The warmth from the mug has seeped into her palm. "We're almost there."

It's only a few-minute drive, and we're barely on the outer limits of town, but it seems like it takes me forever to drive there. I've driven on this road for years, since I was old enough to drive. Hell, Izzy and I used to burn up the gas in the old Ford Ranger I used to drive, spraying gravel and squealing tires out here where no one would complain. There are only a handful of houses, but the houses are newer, more modern. And more pricey, since they're considered the "new part" of Brooksville.

I pull the truck over to the side of the road and kill the engine. This section of the road only has trees lining it on both sides, and the foliage is thick and full, blocking out the sun and creating kaleidoscopic patterns of shadows and light across the gravel.

"What are we doing out here?" Izzy looks around. "It's not really secluded enough to have sex in your truck, if that's what you're thinking."

I burst out laughing, shaking my head. "Christ, Izzy, you're relentless. But, I do like the way you think. C'mon, walk with me."

We climb out of the truck, and I wait in front of it for her, taking her hand in mine before crunching across the gravel and scattered fallen leaves. "Must you always think about sex?" I ask her with a wry grin.

"Oh, you're a fine one to talk." She takes a sip from the mug she brought with her to hide her amusement.

"Good point." I can't deny it. If I'm not buried inside Izzy, kissing her, touching her, then I'm thinking about it. I've never tried to hide that fact. "Can you do me a favor and think about something else with me for a few minutes?"

She turns to me but doesn't stop walking. Her brows arch

high on her forehead. "What else do you want me to think about?" she asks coyly.

"Our future." I give her hand a tight squeeze. "What you want. Where you want to be."

"With you," she says simply, no hesitation. "Wherever you are, that's where I want to be."

A wave of intense heat rolls through me. This woman can set my emotions on fire with only a few words. "I was hoping you'd say that." I bring her hand to my lips and kiss her knuckles tenderly. I stop walking, which forces her to as well. "What about Brooksville?"

She's watching my lips graze the back of her hand like the sight is somehow intoxicating. "If you're in Brooksville, that's where I want to be."

"I was hoping you'd say that, too."

"Why?" she chuckles. "Why all the questions?"

"Because I love you, Isabelle." I place one hand gently on her back and guide her to turn her gaze to the house that's behind her. "And because I bought that."

Izzy turns around to face the house I'm referring to, a large split-level rancher with an attached two-car garage. White brick exterior, a lush yard, and a white fence outlining the perimeter of the property.

"You...bought Sheriff Atkin's house?" She sounds incredulous. "But it wasn't for sale."

Sheriff Atkin has been retired for almost twenty years, but there's no one in Brooksville who doesn't refer to him as the sheriff. "He's moving closer to his daughter in Kansas, Izzy. I bought the place privately from him. Signed the paperwork yesterday morning when I said I was running over to Mom and Dad's house."

She stares at the house as though seeing it for the first time. "You bought Sheriff Atkin's place," she repeats, her gaze never wavering from it. "But...why?"

"Years ago, you told me that house was the kind of house

you wanted to have someday. And, years after that, I told you I would build you the life you deserve, Izzy. Just because you didn't get that text, and just because it took me longer than I thought it would, that doesn't make it any less true. I meant it, Izzy. I want this to be our place. Our own piece of Brooksville."

"You want me to live there—" She points to the house. "With you."

Her dumbfounded expression and repetitiveness are stirring up fear within me. I'm wondering if I misread the signals. "I'd love nothing more," I tell her. I breathe out heavily. "Jesus, Izzy, please tell me what you're thinking."

She stares at the house for a few beats longer, then slowly turns to face me. Her eyes are bright. "It's perfect," she says finally, her voice thick with emotion. "You're perfect," she adds, laughing as a stray tear splashes onto her cheek.

"Oh, Izzy, don't cry." I hug her close to me, forehead to forehead, reaching up to wipe the tear away. "Is it really what you want? I'm beginning to wonder if I overstepped."

She laughs again, a choked sound. "It's amazing, Jace. I mean that. It's more than I've ever wanted, more than I've dreamed of. You know damn well I've fawned over that house since we were kids. It was perfect then, and it's perfect now. I'm just getting all emotional and insane." She chuckles again, a sound mixed with more tears that have started to fall. "You didn't overstep, I swear."

"So, you still love me, and you want to do this crazy thing called life with me from here on in?"

Despite the lackluster way I've phrased it, I can tell she hears the seriousness of what I'm asking, and it brings her up short. "What? Of course, baby. You know I do."

I wipe another tear from her cheek before reaching into the pocket of my jeans and pulling out a navy velvet box. I pop it open with my thumb and hold it out to her. "Have I overstepped now?"

Everything stops. There's no more tears, no more choked laughter, no more sound at all save for the beating of my own heart in my ears. Izzy's eyes are wide, and her mouth is slightly agape.

I use the silence to my advantage, speaking before I lose my nerve. "Izzy, we've been through more than any couple should have to endure. It's been one hell of a rough ride, but one hell of a beautiful one, too. Life led us apart, only to toss us back together when we least expected it. We've made it this far, baby. So, let's go all the way. Isabelle, you're already the love of my life. Do me the honor of being my wife, too."

My voice was already wavering under the weight of my own emotion, so I understood completely when Izzy's mouth opened but no sound came out. Instead, she nodded her head furiously, then broke into a full-fledged crying fit as she flung her arms around me. Tears stung my eyes, but she was in my arms and nodding was a good sign, so I gave her the time she needed to compose herself.

Frankly, I needed it, too.

"Yes," she sniffed when she finally pulled back and she'd calmed a bit. "So much, yes. I want nothing more than to be your wife."

I kissed her mouth hard, an unspoken promise of what was to come. "You make me happy, Izzy. So damn happy."

"You make me happy, too." She shakes her head as I slip the three-stone diamond ring on her finger.

Past, present, and future. For me, Izzy is all of those things.

"I still can't believe we're here," she breathes out. "Doing this. Being *us*."

"We were always *us*, Izzy." I give her a soft smile. "Miles and years couldn't change that. That's why I came back. To make sure it wasn't just me that felt the pull of...us. I told myself I needed closure. But what I really needed was you."

Izzy sighed audibly as I touched her face, leaning into my

hand. "I needed you, too. Even if I didn't want to admit it to myself. I think my heart always knew, though."

I lean in, running my lips across her jaw. "Wine after whisky," I whisper against her skin.

She smiles, as that phrase has become an inside joke between us. Something that so accurately describes the fire between us, an intense burning unmatched by the touch of anyone else. "I've never been a fan of wine, anyway," she whispers. "Take me home, Jace."

I smile down into her pretty brown eyes. "We are home, Izzy," I remind her. "We're together."

ABOUT THE AUTHOR

Cass Kincaid writes steamy romance stories, creates HEAs, and loves every damn minute of it. She LOVES love, and she's a hopeless romantic. Oh, and she has a thing for sexy, sarcastic fictional boyfriends, but don't we all?

ABOUT THE PUBLISHER

EverLust Books is an imprint of Harbor Lane Books, LLC. We are a US-based independent digital publisher of steamy contemporary romance to erotic fiction.

Connect with EverLust Books on our website www.everlustbooks.com and TikTok, Instagram, and Twitter @everlustbooks.

ALSO BY CASS KINCAID

www.ingramcontent.com/pod-product-compliance
Lightning Source LLC
LaVergne TN
LVHW041633070526
838199LV00052B/3336